Dedicated in loving memory
to Miriam Sper Magdol ז"ל,
whose flame will burn on
long after her passing.

—E.S.

SCHOLASTIC, CARTWHEEL BOOKS, and associated logos
are trademarks and/or registered trademarks of Scholastic Inc.

Library of Congress Cataloging-in-Publication Data available

ISBN 0-439-56704-1

10 9 8 7 6 5 4 3 2 1   03 04 05 06 07

Printed in China

First printing, October 2003

Hanukkah

A Counting Book

IN ENGLISH, HEBREW, AND YIDDISH

by **Emily Sper**

SCHOLASTIC INC.

New York Toronto London Auckland Sydney
Mexico City New Delhi Hong Kong Buenos Aires

In winter, when the days are short and the nights are long, the Jewish people celebrate Hanukkah — The Festival of Lights.

Hanukkah is a joyous holiday. We light candles and sing songs. There are potato pancakes and jelly doughnuts to eat. With our spinning tops and coins we play games.

When we celebrate Hanukkah, we use many Hebrew and Yiddish words. We eat LATKES, spin DREIDELS *(dreydleh)*, are given Hanukkah GELT, and light candles in a Hanukkah MENORAH. These words are all in an English dictionary!

Even though *menorah* is a Hebrew word, in Modern Hebrew there is a special word for a Hanukkah menorah. Can you say *ha-noo-kee-YAH*?

Hebrew and Yiddish have a sound that we don't make in English. Try saying "huh" while clearing your throat. Make this sound when you see an "h" printed in green in this book. Once you can say "huh" you will be able to say "Hanukkah" in Hebrew (*ha-noo-KAH*) and Yiddish (*HA-nik-e*).

And when you are able to say *HA-nik-e*, try *HA-nik-e LAY-hter* (Hanukkah candlestick) and *HA-nik-e lempl* (Hanukkah lamp).

The Hebrew and Yiddish languages are very different from each other, but both are written in the Hebrew alphabet. The pronunciation of every Hebrew and Yiddish word in this book is spelled out in English.

Stress the syllables shown in CAPITAL letters and you will be able to sound out all of the words — even if you don't know how to read the Hebrew alphabet.

In Hebrew every noun is either masculine or feminine (male or female), even if it is a table or crayon. And numbers have to match the thing being counted. That's why the word for "one" is *ehad* when you say "one boy" and *ahat* when you say "one girl." In this book, the words printed in blue are masculine; those in pink, feminine.

■ ENGLISH

■ HEBREW masculine (male)

■ HEBREW feminine (female)

■ YIDDISH

PRONUNCIATION KEY

a or ah: as in **ma** or **pa**
ay: as in **bye-bye**
e or eh: as in **egg**
ee: as in **bee**
ey: as in **hey**
h: as in **Ha-noo-KAH**
i: as in **it**
o: in Hebrew, as in **go**
o: in Yiddish, between **awe** and **won**
oo: as in **moo**
s: as in **so**
sh: as in **ship**

worker candle

(sha-MASH) שַׁמָּשׁ

(SHA-mes) שמש

With the *sha-MASH,*

light one more

candle every night

to make EIGHT

candles burning

bright . . .

or NINE candles

if you count

the *SHA-mes*!

one Hanukkah menorah / Hanukkah lamp

חֲנֻכִּיָּה אַחַת (ha-noo-kee-YAH a-HAT)

איין חנוכה-לעמפל (eyn HA-nik-e LEM-pl)

איין חנוכה-לייכטער (eyn HA-nik-e LAYH-ter)

one

(e-HAD) אֶחָד

(a-HAT) אַחַת

(eyns) איינס

1

two jelly doughnuts

(shtey soof-ga-nee-YOT) שְׁתֵּי סוּפְגָּנִיּוֹת

(tsvey PONTSH-kes) צוויי פּאָנטשקעס

two

(SHNA-yeem) שְׁנַיִם

(SHTA-yeem) שְׁתַּיִם

(tsvey) צוויי

2

three

3

(shlo-SHAH) שְׁלֹשָׁה

(sha-LOSH) שָׁלֹשׁ

(dray) דרײַ

Watch the Hebrew
letters on the dreidel
spin, spin, spin . . .
נ – nun
ג – GI-mel
ה – hey
שׁ – shin

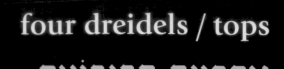

four dreidels / tops

אַרְבָּעָה סְבִיבוֹנִים
(ar-ba-AH s'vee-vo-NEEM)

פִיר דריידלער
(fir DREYD-leh)

נֵס (nes)
miracle

גָדוֹל (ga-DOL)
great

הָיָה (ha-YAH)
happened

שָׁם (sham)
there

Mattathias

Judah
the Maccabee

Eleazar

six heroes

שִׁשָּׁה גִבּוֹרִים
(shee-SHAH gee-bo-REEM)

זעקס גיבורים
(zeks gi-BOY-rim)

Jonathan

Simon

Johanan

five

(ha-mee-SHAH) חֲמִשָּׁה

(ha-MESH) חָמֵשׁ

(finf) פינף

5

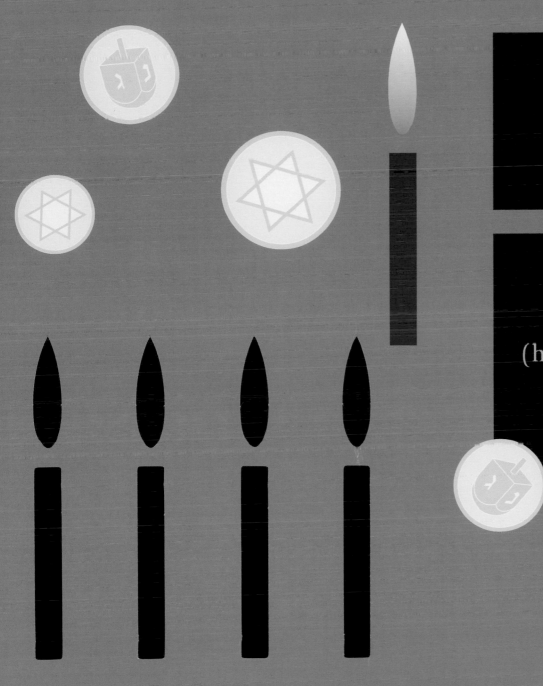

gelt / money

כֶּסֶף (KE-sef)

גֿעלט (gelt)

five coins

חֲמֵשׁ מַטְבְּעוֹת
(ha-MESH mat-be-OT)

פֿינף מטבעות
(finf mat BEY-cs)

four

(ar-ba-AH) אַרְבָּעָה

(AR-bah) אַרְבַּע

(fir) פיר

4

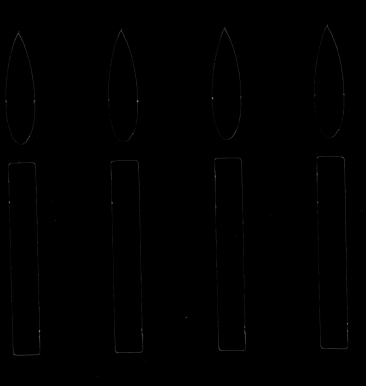

six

(shee-SHAH) שִׁשָּׁה

(shesh) שֵׁשׁ

(zeks) זעקס

6

seven
potato pancakes

שֶׁבַע לְבִיבוֹת
(SHE-vah lev-ee-VOT)

זיבן לאַטקעס
(zibn LAT-kes)

six

(shee-SHAH) שִׁשָּׁה

(shesh) שֵׁשׁ

(zeks) זעקס

6

**seven
potato pancakes**

שֶׁבַע לְבִיבוֹת
(SHE-vah lev-ee-VOT)

זיבן לאַטקעס
(zibn LAT-kes)

seven

(sheev-AH) שִׁבְעָה

(SHE-vah) שֶׁבַע

(zibn) זיבן

7

eight nights

שְׁמוֹנָה לֵילוֹת

(shmo-NAH ley-LOT)

אכט נעכט

(aht neht)

eight candles

שְׁמוֹנָה נֵרוֹת

(shmo-NAH ney-ROT)

אכט ליכטלעך

(aht LIHT-leh)

eight

(shmo-NAH) שְׁמוֹנָה

(SHMO-neh) שְׁמוֹנָה

(aht) אכט

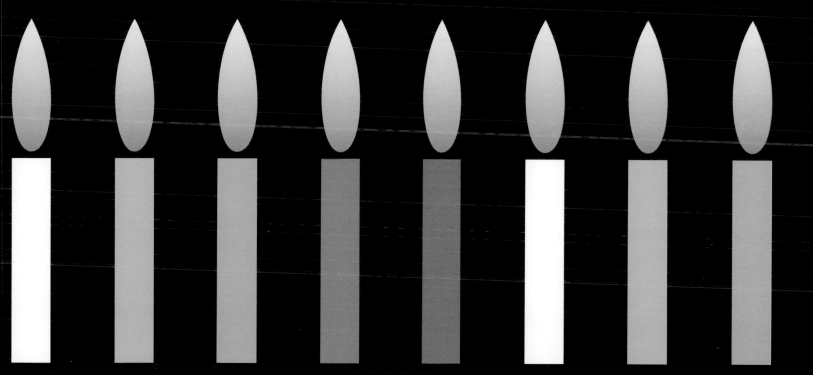

Happy Hanukkah!

חַג חֲנֻכָּה שָׂמֵחַ!
(hag ha-noo-KAH sa-MEY-ah)

גוט יום-טובֿ!
(gut YON-tev)

Growing up, my sister and I both wanted to light the candles on the last night. That meant we took turns. Some years I had the first, third, fifth, and seventh nights. Other years I was lucky enough to get the second, fourth, sixth, and EIGHTH nights.

On each of *my* nights I picked out a different set of colored candles. Before placing the candles in the Hanukkah menorah, I laid them on the table and moved them around until a pattern pleased me. Only then did I place the candles in the menorah.

After lighting the candles, my family ate latkes with applesauce on top. Latkes with sour cream also taste great. Did you ever wonder why we eat latkes to celebrate Hanukkah? Here's a hint: The Maccabees found oil in the Temple. Can you figure it out? Latkes are cooked in oil!

And so are *soof-ga-nee-YOT,* special jelly doughnuts eaten in Israel for Hanukkah. When I grew up I moved there. Now I live in Boston, where I am very happy eating both latkes and *soof-ga-nee-YOT!*

For me, the best thing about Hanukkah is that it comes EVERY year.

—*Emily Sper*

THE HANUKKAH STORY

Many years ago, when the Syrian-Greeks ruled Ancient Israel they put statues of Greek gods in every town. The people were told that if they didn't pray to the Greek gods they would be punished. One man refused. His name was Mattathias and his sons were Judah, Eleazar, Simon, Jonathan, and Johanan. Judah was called "the Maccabee" and his band of fighters, the "Maccabees." They revolted against the Syrian-Greeks, using shields to protect themselves from the spears of their enemies.

Even when the Syrian-Greeks attacked on ELEPHANTS they couldn't stop the Maccabee rebellion. Judah and the Maccabees drove the Syrian-Greeks out of Jerusalem! They were HEROES.

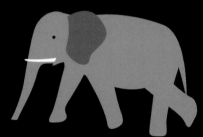

After the fighting ended, the Maccabees cleaned the Temple from top to bottom and took out the statues of the Greek gods. Now the temple could again be used by the Jewish people as a place to pray.

The Temple was *rededicated* as a place of prayer. HANUKKAH means "dedication" in Hebrew. To dedicate the Temple, the Maccabees put oil in the MENORAH and lit it. The menorah is an ancient Jewish symbol. The menorah in the Temple had only *seven* branches — three branches on each side and one in the middle.

A legend tells us that the Maccabees found only enough sacred oil to burn for one day. But there was a miracle: The oil burned for **EIGHT NIGHTS** and eight days! During that time the Maccabees were able to get more pure oil to keep the menorah burning. The Hanukkah menorah has nine candles, one for each of the eight nights and one with which to light the others. For many years people lit oil in their Hanukkah menorahs, but today we usually light **CANDLES**.

It was a miracle! The letters on a **DREIDEL** are the first letters of the Hebrew words *nes ga-DOL ha-YAH sham* — a great miracle happened there. The miracle of Hanukkah happened in Ancient Israel. So if you live in Israel, a great miracle happened HERE . . . not THERE. That's why Israeli *s'vee-vo NEEM* have the letters *nun, GI-mel, hey,* and *PEY. Pey* is the first letter of the word *PO* which means "here." In Yiddish the letters *nun, GI-mel, hey,* and *shin* tell us how to play a game. Players sit in a circle. Everyone begins with some pennies, puts one into the center, and takes a turn spinning the dreidel. If it lands with the letter *nun* face-up, the player does nothing (*nit*); on *GI-mel,* takes all pennies in the center (*gants*); on *hey,* takes half (*halb*); on *shin,* all players put one penny in the center (*shtel*).

(nit) ניט
not

(gants) גאַנץ
everything

(halb) האַלב
half

(shtel) שטעל
put

POTATO PANCAKES and **JELLY DOUGHNUTS** remind us of the miracle of the oil. They taste SO good we sometimes forget about the miracle!

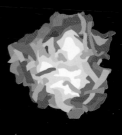

It is a Hanukkah tradition to give children the gift of money. At one time, coins were gold and silver. Today **HANUKKAH GELT** is often thin pieces of chocolate wrapped in gold foil!

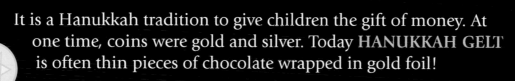